J H   N E L S O N

DANGEROUS
Thrills

Dangerous Thrills
Copyright © 2025 JH Nelson

This new adult contemporary romance is recommended for readers 18+ due to mature content.

Cover design by 1231 Publishing

ISBN: 978-0-6451315-4-3

Second Edition - March 2025

Published by J. H. Nelson

ACKNOWLEDGEMENTS

There are so many people that have helped to bring this book to life. If I were to name all of you individually, we would be here for days, so I will try to keep it short. If I forget anyone, please accept my most humble apologies, and know that I am grateful to all the beautiful people surrounding me, lifting me up and helping me reach my dreams.

To my husband, Clinton, who has spent many a night sorting out dinner for all of us, watching movies alone while I tapped away at the keyboard in the background, madly getting my words and thoughts down on the screen. You have been there to remind me in my weaker moments why I continue this journey and that I am loved always.

To all of my family and friends. You have all contributed to help me achieve this dream of mine.

Reading through countless pieces of writing, offering your feedback and words of encouragement. spurring me on and listening to me waffle on about my characters when I needed to voice plot ideas. These moments have all helped shape and fine-tune my writing skills into something I am proud to put out into the world today. Thank you.

A special mention to some specific people who read through and helped bring Dangerous Thrills to life are: Kristy, Amy, and Freya. Your encouraging feedback shone light on different areas of this story that needed more attention, less detail or tweaking of sentence structure.

While I have made many friends among the writing community, all of whom have taught me things along the way and who I hold dearly, there are three women who have opened their arms to me and held my hand through it all. Dee, Jodie, Fi, what can I say but wow! Jodie… The meeting of a like-minded stranger for lunch and a chat in a coffee shop, what feels like a bazillion moons ago, was the beginning of a beautiful friendship that quickly grew in numbers with the introduction to Dee and Fi.

You ladies have mentored and encouraged me at every turn and with every new storyline I presented.

The knowledge and talent you all have shared and taught me throughout this journey is so much more than just writing skills. So, thank you. I hope we have many more lunch/dinner outings and swapping of writing pieces together in our future.

Last but certainly not least, I want to extend my warmest, deepest, and humblest thank you and appreciation to all of you, my readers! Without your ongoing support and encouraging messages of love and enjoyment whilst reading my stories, I wouldn't be where I am today.

Thank you!

ONE

It happened in an instant. One minute he was filling the car with petrol, the next, Peter was ten years old again, plucking up the courage to kiss her soft lips while she sat cross-legged, eyes closed on the grass in his mother's front yard. The memory ripped through him like a bolt of electricity. How long had it been? Why was she back? How long was she staying? Questions hounded him, each one succeeding the last.

As she finished refuelling her own vehicle, Elizabeth's gaze lifted and Peter spun away from her, focusing on his own petrol nozzle, worried she'd spied his grimy-self. Sweat broke out along his hands. *What the fuck?* What was going on? He wasn't the same pimple-faced schoolboy who'd fallen in love with her. How the hell was she able to invoke such a response, after all these years?

With his eyes glued to the car he was filling— another one for his mate, Tommy—he pondered how best to play this out without her seeing him. The pump was about to stop, and then he'd have to go in and pay. He hadn't seen her fancy SUV drive off yet, so she was obviously still inside. *Click*. He was out of time. It was inevitable that he was going to cross her path. With a quick breath, he hung up the hose and hoped she wouldn't recognise him. It could happen. Maybe.

Passing her SUV, Peter couldn't help but notice the badges. Cars were his thing, after all. It was top of the line. *Of course it is… some things never change!* Inside the shop, Peter glanced around searching for her, but the place was empty besides the cashier. He paid for his petrol, feeling a mixture of relief and annoyance that he'd escaped detection, when the pivot door to the public restrooms opened.

Like metal to a magnet, his eyes were lured to hers. He saw her falter. Everything about her screamed 'confidence'. If it weren't for her miss-step, he wouldn't have even known he'd affected her. But he *did* see it.

"Pete? Oh, my god. Is it really you?"

"Beth. Wow. Long time no see. What brings you

back to Hellhole-Ville?" *Play it cool, Pete.* He thought to himself.

Elizabeth laughed. "I haven't heard it called that in about ten years. It's Liz these days."

Peter offered a tight smile small and the slightest nod of his head. It was exactly like her to change her name to fit in. "So. That your fancy beast I see parked out there? That model's got the turbo, hasn't it? They're s'posed to go like shit off a shovel, I'm told."

Again, Elizabeth laughed. "That it does. Sadly, though, not mine. It's a rental. I'm staying at mum's. Maybe we could catch up sometime and I'll show you what she can do." There was a teasing glint in her eye. It lit a fire in Peter's belly.

"Drive it like you stole it, hey, Bee?" He hadn't meant to use the old pet name and cursed internally after it slipped past his lips.

Elizabeth glanced at her feet. With a soft smile, she replied. "That was a long time ago. I wouldn't know that girl if I saw her. No longer clinging to bad boys on the back of their motorcycles. Nor stealing their motorcycles out from under them. Thank goodness, I got smarter with age… Well, that and the community service sentence might have played a solid part in my coming-of-wisdom as well." She chuckled sarcastically.

"You know that wasn't me, right? I would never've dumped you in it, I swear." Peter's chest tightened with the ancient anguish rising from the dead. Elizabeth rested a hand on his arm.

"Relax, Pete. I knew then that you'd never stitch me. We were solid. Truth is, it doesn't matter anymore. Whoever squealed did me a favour. If it weren't for the threat of being locked up in prison, I'd never have straightened up. These days I make friends, not enemies."

"We were friends."

"Sure were." The emotion and memory in her voice did strange things to Peter's insides. He stepped back to make his retreat.

"Right. Well, nice to see you. Might catch you again if you're staying in town for a while."

"I'd like that." Peter heard Elizabeth reply as he dashed safely back towards the fresh air of outside. He needed to clear his mind of the intoxicatingly delicious scent of her perfume and climb back into the car that would remove him from her and all the haunting memories.

TWO

Working for Tom was a pisser. He loved Tom and he was grateful for everything he'd done. That wasn't the issue. The issue was that honest money was hard. He slogged his guts out for peanuts. But it kept him out of trouble. Mostly.

Peter lay half in a car, working upside down, disassembling a dash when he heard Tom arguing with someone. He listened, but their words were muffled. Realisation dawned when he heard his name, and it took all of his good sense not to fly out of the car. Instead, he curled up, keeping his feet out of sight as best he could, just like Tom had asked him to. He hated letting someone else take the heat for him while he cowered in hiding.

The discussion ended. Tom came and leaned

against the open car door. Peter let out a breath and unwound himself up and out of the passenger footwell. Blood rushed away from his pounding head, making him dizzy for a minute. "Who?" was all he asked.

"It was John." Tom said seriously.

"Jesus. Now Johnno's in on it?" The news hit him like a punch in the gut.

"Looks like." Tom slapped a huge brother-like palm on Peter's shoulder. "Hey, man, I got your back. And I can protect you here, but you gotta go to the cops. I can't keep you safe after you leave this shed every night. Think about it, 'ey?"

"Someone going to the cops is what got me in this mess in the first place, Tommy. No coppers!" Peter frowned, shaking his head and staring at the shop floor.

"What then? Huh? They'll kill you, Pete. And for what? It wasn't even you. Why're you still protecting her?"

Clenching and unclenching his fists, Peter's emotions warred beneath the surface. With a heavy sigh, he pinched the bridge of his nose to keep his tone even. "Because I know it wasn't her! And if anyone's gonna go down for this, then better it be me than her. She's made something of herself. Now, no more talk about coppers, yeah?"

"Whatever, man. I don't know if you're trying to be noble or plain stupid, but dead is dead. Just remember that. I'd be asking myself if she's worth it."

Peter felt Tom's eyes following him around the shop after that. He should explain. Tell him that she's back. He needed to untwist the feelings in his own mind first. With the last customer gone, Peter helped Tom close up before taking off for the night. It had been a long day. So much had happened since he walked through the heavy roller door at six that morning. He would give anything for a beer, but he'd have to settle for a nice cold shower. Driving home, Peter's thoughts drifted back to Elizabeth. *Why is she back? What does she want?* He thought about Johnno. Reece must have something over him, Peter decided. But what? Peter couldn't think of a single thing. Peter couldn't imagine Johnno switching sides of his own making. But then… some people just couldn't be trusted. How many times had life taught him that?

Peter turned his borrowed vehicle towards his mother's house, telling himself it was to fill her in about Johnno, but in the back of his mind, Elizabeth's face emerged.

Pulling in behind his mother's crummy hatchback, Peter noted the shiny SUV in next door's driveway winking at him under the last of the sun's rays before dark. He stared for a minute before forcing his dirty, aching body to move.

"Mum, it's me, Pete." He heard movement behind the door and then the click of the deadbolt releasing before it opened. Peter's heart broke a little every time he came back here. The fear he'd caused her throughout the years had aged her prematurely. He wished he could make it all go away for her. Years ago, when he'd tried to convince her to get out of town and start fresh somewhere new, leaving him behind forever, she'd flatly refused his offer stating a bunch of thugs weren't running her out of her hometown. Remembering her tiny five foot three inches frame all feisty and righteous, Peter smiled. The woman had grit. He'd give her that.

"Hey, Mum." Peter opened his arms to her, and she obliged despite his grease-stricken clothes.

"This is a nice surprise. Have you eaten?" She stretched up to pat his tall bulk. Peter chuckled, shaking his head. Typical mum... always trying to feed him. She ushered him inside, heading for the stove. "Sit, sit. I'll make you something. What do you want? An omelette? Macaroni and cheese? Name your poison," she smiled lovingly. He sighed. *I don't deserve her kindness.*

Chowing down on a delicious omelette filled with all the trimmings, Peter watched his mother sitting across from him with a peaceful look about her face, sipping a cup of tea. He was about to shatter that calm once again, and the knowledge pained him.

"Mum, the reason I came over—"

"I know, dear. Isn't it wonderful that she's back in town? I was going to call you, but then you showed up here."

"What? No, Mum... I'm here because I got another visit... at the shed today."

"Oh." She reached for the amethyst pendant she'd worn around her neck since before Peter could remember and worried it nervously along its chain.

"It was Johnno, Mum. Reece's gettin' more crafty and he's corrupting people closer to home. I don't have a clue what he said to get inside Johnno's head, but I know Johnno wouldn't be swayed easily, so we need to be extra careful. Don't trust anyone, Mum... I don't know who he'll get to next." Peter sighed. The look in his mother's eyes was killing him. "Mum, I want you to promise me if he or anyone else comes here or calls you on the phone, I want you to ring the police. Straight away. They'll look after you." Peter saw his mother's jaw clench.

The hard set of her shoulders told him she would not follow his advice. *She would rather die herself than call the coppers and seal my fate. Or Johnno's.* They had been over all this before. Peter knew there was no point in arguing with her. Once her mind was made up, there would be no changing it.

THREE

Saturday morning arrived and Peter—unable to sleep since learning about Johnno—came up with a plan. He needed to head back to where it all began. A place where only distant memories and the ghosts of his past lingered. It was risky. It could definitely get him killed. But if, by some miracle, it worked, it might free him. With the window down, wind jostled the hair at his ear while the sun heated his neck and arm. He squinted and finger-combed the hair back into place.

No matter which way he worked the logistics through in his mind, Peter always came back to the same stumbling block. He needed someone else's help. He couldn't physically move cars to *and* from without a pickup person at the other end.

Frustration gnawed at him as he thumped the steering wheel. "God damn it!" He yelled to no one. The idea seemed so flawless at two am the night before.

Elizabeth, though back in town, was straight down the line these days. Involving Tommy was a terrible solution. His employer and only friend, the one who had helped him clean up and who'd made something more of himself—*like Bee*—he had a lot to lose and nothing to gain by helping a mate do a dodgy. With Johnno out of the question now and any of his old contacts considered untrustworthy at best, Peter faced few other options. He dialled Tommy's number, the ringtone surrounded him on the hands-free speakers.

"Yo! Didn't you get enough of my ugly mug all week that you gotta call me on your day off?" Tom laughed through the phone, making Peter smile in spite of himself.

"And miss these cheery pep talks... no way!" Peter turned serious then "Nuh, listen, mate, I got something to run by you and I reckon you ain't gonna like it, but I want you to hear me out before you say anything, yeah?"

"Mmm, that sounds ominous. I make no promises."

"Here's the thing. If I can pull enough money

together, I reckon I can buy Reece off. Do a deal with him in return for my freedom. For good. Now, as much as I appreciate everything you've done for me and love looking like I've shacked up with the grease gun in the back of your shop every day... I can't save the kind of money I'd need just working at the shop. I need it fast enough to get him off my tail before he kills me. I need—"

"You need a loan? I'm sorry, man—"

"I can't take your money, Tommy, and even if I could... you don't have enough." Peter sighed, unable to believe what he was about to do. "I'm gonna do one last run. I *need* to do one last run." Peter stared out the windshield, waiting for Tom to respond. The silence was all he heard. "Tommy?"

"Have you completely lost your mind? What about your work at the shop? What about your poor—"

"What the hell?" Peter interrupted him. Up ahead, he spotted the signature look of Reece's work driving erratically. "Tommy, hold on a sec... something's goin' on." Peter dropped back a gear and put his foot down, weaving through the traffic to get a closer look. "Tommy, what's Reece driving these days?"

"Pfft, changes daily. Last I heard, it was a sports car. Silver, I think. Might've been gun-metal. Why?

What's going on?"

"Let me guess, Johnno was driving a black Typhoon look-alike when he came into work, wasn't he?"

"That'd be the one. What're you doing, Pete?"

"Not me. *Them*. Reece and Johnno have Bee boxed in along Adelaide Road." Unconsciously, Peter reverted back to her pet name as her safety gained his focus.

"Wait, what? Since when is Beth here? And if you knew this, why didn't you tell me?"

"I only found out the day Johnno came to the shop and then, well… Johnno happened and I never got back around to it."

"When you went to the servo… I knew something was up with you! I'm getting in the car. Which end of Adelaide you at?"

"Just passing the Fisherman's Inn on my left now. If you can get to the corner of Adelaide and Mary in four minutes, you should just about side-swipe us."

"Perfect. I'll be there in two."

"Good. Beth's in a black SUV. I'm gonna try to call her—if her number's still the same—but if not, we need to try to ditch these parasites and steer her towards…where? The old fishing docks?"

"Too isolated. The Plaza. Right near the eatery

entrance where all the security cameras are. Reece won't get his face out anywhere near there."

"Perfect. I'll call her now. Get on Adelaide and keep an eye open. We're coming at speed."

Using the steering wheel controls this time, Peter searched through his contacts, looking for Elizabeth's number. Saved under Bee; it didn't take him long. It rang. Peter was both surprised and relieved when he heard the voice that was still so familiar to his ears after all this time.

"Hey, Pete." She was trying to sound offhand, but Peter heard the tension behind her words. He gripped his steering wheel tighter, rage engulfing him. *If I ever get my hands on Johnno, I will rip him in half!*

"You see the red HSV coming up in your rear-vision mirror?" He flashed his lights at her. "I'm coming, hold on."

"How? You were in a white Lexus the other—"

"I like to keep it interesting. Never mind all that. See the silver sports on your right? That's Reece. You remember him, right? Unhinged psychopath who removed three of Johnno's fingers because he flicked a cigarette at his feet. *That* Reece. And the black wannabe Typhoon behind you… Yeah, that's Johnno, who is apparently working for said psycho these days. I have to assume they've mended their differences. Tommy is on the way and we're gonna split them up. You need to head to the Plaza. I want you to park right in front of the eatery doors. You remember the one? That entrance is crawling with security. I want you to stay in your car and lock the doors if we get split up. If you can safely get to the eatery, do it, but go straight inside. I'll find you, ok. Don't come out by yourself!"

"I don't understand. What's going on? What do they—"

"I know you don't. I'll explain everything, but right now, I need you to put your foot down. You need to get ahead of that Subaru and the second you are, cut across and hook a right onto Vincent. Time to see if that turbo of yours is everything they say it is. If Reece makes the turn, I'll be right behind you both, but if not, I'll stay with him and try to lure him away." Peter watched as Elizabeth measured her timing. He saw Reece swerve dangerously towards an innocent vehicle in the left lane. Just when Peter was about to tell Elizabeth to hook it, she did. It was as if they were thinking as one. Peter saw Reece followed her around the corner, narrowly missing a pedestrian. *Damn it!* Johnno too, navigated the turn. Peter never let more than a Coke can worth of air get between his bonnet and Johnno's tailpipes. *What's your next move, Johnno?*

Don't forget who taught you how to drive, punk!

"You still with me, Pete? I can't see if you made it around. I didn't lose them. Unfortunately."

"Yup, I'm riding Johnno's exhaust gas. Don't think he likes me much. Thought you were gonna roll your pretty SUV around that bend, though. Corners like a bag of shit! Think we'll cross 'rally car' off its list of specs. Next time, get something smaller… something that's lower to the ground and got big feet on it."

"Sure thing, boss. Didn't think I'd be needing a getaway car though when I hired it. Just saying. Besides… you know sports cars have never been my style. It's hard to find a rental car 'ute' with all the trimmings, you know?" Elizabeth's voice oozed with mischief despite the stressful situation the pair found themselves in. Peter realised then that she had it, too. The disease. She was still the same reckless thrill-seeker she'd always been. Addicted to the danger, the speed, all of it. At complete ease, making idle chit-chat while punishing a vehicle to the brink.

"Yeah, yeah. Concentrate, Beth. We're not playing with amateurs here. I don't think we're gonna shake 'em. Head for the eatery, but take it easy. Coppers love to hang out there. Don't stop rolling until you're parked or Reece'll nab ya.

Tommy's all ready for ya. He just texted. Pull in on his passenger side. Reece won't stop in that carpark but I can't guess what Johnno will do. I'm a half dozen cars behind if I don't gain more on the merging lane. I'll see you in a sec." Peter disconnected the call.

FOUR

Sitting across from her, Peter saw disbelief etched all over Elizabeth's face. Was he wrong to believe her innocent, so blindly? What if she'd just gotten better at lying? He was exhausted. He didn't have the energy to open this shit-show right now. There were bigger issues.

Peter scanned the eatery nervously. One could never be one hundred percent certain of the lengths Reece might go to for revenge.

"Let's get outta here. Go for a drive. This place is clearing out and I don't want to give Reece or Johnno a window of opportunity. Come with me?" Even as he said the words, Peter's better judgement screamed at him not to do this. Not to invite her into his car, or his life. Elizabeth was quicksand.

"Sure."

The confined space of the car was intimate and brought with it an awkwardness between them. They travelled this way for some time before Elizabeth broke the silence.

"This car suits you. Your personality." She smiled, looking around its interior.

"What do you know about my personality? You've been MIA for the past seven years." He'd been trying for offhand, but his words came out cold and critical. She didn't need to know that the car wasn't his.

"I wasn't MIA, as you so put it. You knew where I was. Don't go acting all cut up on me now. You never came knocking." Elizabeth rolled her eyes and gazed out the passenger window. "I was such a stupid fool back then." Peter couldn't see her expression. *Is she talking about us? Reece? Is she suggesting that she's stupid because she wanted me to follow her and I didn't? She must know I wanted to. Hell, I nearly did, despite her silence. She knew! Unless she never read my letter. Would someone wanting, not read a letter? Unless…*

The wheels spun in Peter's brain as he revisited the painful memories he'd long since buried. It all came together. How could he have been so naïve to think she would keep her word?

"You don't know." It wasn't a question. "You never got my letter... Finally, it all makes—"

"What letter?" Elizabeth interrupted. Turning on him with a stare so cold, he felt it.

"Exactly!" Peter's eyes left the road as he slapped a hand against the steering wheel in confirmation. "I wrote to you after you took off. I begged your mum to give me your address, but she refused. Said she'd forward it on and if you wanted to, you'd write back... you knew my address. Only, she never sent it to you and in all these years... that never occurred to me, until right now." Peter scrubbed at the stubble lining his jaw. *You bloody idiot!*

"What did it say?" Came Elizabeth's sad voice.

"Hardly matters now, does it?" He steered the car onto the overgrown dirt driveway of the property, bringing the locked up old aeroplane hangar into view.

"Now is exactly why it *does* matter!"

"You want to read it? You'll need to ask your mother if she kept it or chucked it in the bin! We're here." Peter killed the engine and leapt from his seat, furious at himself for inviting Elizabeth to come with him and for ever trusting her mother, a woman he thought he knew.

"Why the fuck did you bring me here? This isn't funny, Pete."

"Relax. I was on my way out here when I came across a damsel getting harassed by a pair of first class jackasses. You're welcome, by the way." Peter retrieved a sharp rock near the front wheel, tossed it into the air twice and then launched it off into the scrub to avoid a tyre puncture. "Don't tell me you're still afraid that ghosts lurk here?" Peter smirked. His amusement, obvious. The boys had always teased her that the shed's creaks and groans were the spirits of the property's old owners haunting the dwelling.

Peter meandered this way and that, looking through the knee-high grass where car paraphernalia lay like dilapidated old headstones of a deserted graveyard. Metal had rusted and seized. Plastic mouldings lay destroyed by the harsh sun and weather. There was nothing salvageable outside.

Reaching the hangar, Peter wrestled the stiff door open. Its metal rollers groaned in protest after years of sitting sedentary. Inside was hidden in shadow, the only light being that which shone in from behind him. Whirlybirds circled on the roof, throwing patterns against the concrete floor. Peter squinted, letting his eyes adjust to the darkness.

Work benches were littered with everything from tools and caulking guns to empty beer cans. The place was like a time capsule. Old memories stirred and Peter saw flashbacks of his youth. The fun they'd had. The adrenaline rush they lived under constantly. The addiction of it, as dangerous as any other. And towards the end... The bloodshed. Peter's heart raced and he worked to keep his breath even.

At the far end of the bench, the old stereo sat hidden beneath a thick layer of dust. The relic would've been unrecognisable to anyone who didn't know it was there. Another flashback sparked from his subconscious. He slammed the lid down tight on the memory.

Peter heard the crunch of gravel as Elizabeth stepped close behind him. One step and he could have her in his arms. Now, where had that come from? Peter stalked into the shed, giving his brain space to think clearly.

"It looks exactly like I remember," echoed Elizabeth's quiet voice. "So many memories."

"Yep. Of all things illegal," Peter replied sarcastically.

"Not everything that happened here was against the law," Elizabeth rebutted.

"Oh yeah? Name me one thing that wasn't." Why had he challenged her? The flashback came haunting again of two young teenagers, full of booze and sharing a joint. Elizabeth sitting up on the workbench among the grime. In her ripped jeans and tank top, Peter had always thought she looked hotter than any supermodel. She'd been laughing at something and swayed forward drunkenly. Saving her from falling, somehow Peter landed between her open thighs, and next thing they were kissing like their young lives depended on it. Music rumbling from the stereo.

Peter's cock grew hard in his jeans, clearly remembering the old memory with equal enjoyment. He gritted his teeth and clamped the lock shut on his vault of all things 'Bee' and moved quickly to escape her. Deep in the darkness, he adjusted himself, away from those rich chocolate-brown eyes.

"Ok, you got me. I guess it *was* all illegal." Came Elizabeth's delayed response. Peter smirked, his back to her. There was no way she could forget any more than he could. So she was playing this game then. Well, that was fine with him.

Peter roamed the over-sized hangar looking for anything to inspire him. He was out of the business. He needed a completely new look if he was to pull this off. Anything resembling his old style would tip Reece off. Reece would kill him without question. Peter needed to think smarter. Reece had grown cocky with no competition, but if there was one thing Peter knew for sure, it was that cockiness bred carelessness. Peter knew that if he kept his nose low, he might just pull this off.

Crouched down on his haunches, Peter stared. A bright yellow spoiler kit sat in the corner of the vast space, laid out on rags. Pre-painted and ready for installation. His signature design, bold colour kits against stock colour bodies. He'd had a stream of customers so long chasing his 'look,' he'd begun taking larger 'under the table' payments for anyone wanting to jump the queue. He shook his head now in disgrace. His arrogance back then had a lot to answer for. Maybe he deserved to die for what he'd done. Maybe Johnno had every right to turn on him the way he had. The image of his mum, wearing a black dress, crying into a hanky came to mind. He felt as if his heart was being ripped from his flesh. No, he had to do this, for her, if not himself. He needed a plan. Fast.

"So, what are we doing here, anyway?"

"Just lookin' around," came Peter's nonchalant reply.

"Yeah, 'cause it's such a scenic place. Come on, Pete. Are you forgetting... I'm the one they had boxed in this morning? What're you scheming up in that pretty head of yours?"

"That's one it's never been called."

"Ten points for diversion tactics, but I know you. I'm your friend, not your enemy."

"To be honest, Beth… I don't know who's my friend and who's my enemies anymore. Lots has changed in the seven years you've been gone. I'm not the kid you knew anymore." Peter rose, his back still to Elizabeth. He contemplated. Swivelling a loose nut from the shed floor around in his fingers. It was true. He couldn't remember the last time he'd felt this unsure about the people in his life. If Johnno could switch sides, there was no telling who'd be next.

"I see you, Pete. Don't do it."

Peter flinched at Elizabeth's soft plea beside him. In his preoccupation, he hadn't heard her move closer. She rested her hand on his shoulder and massaged it gently. His eyes slid shut while allowing himself to enjoy her touch. It wasn't long before reality crowded in and he stepped away. "Whatever it is… don't do it, Pete."

"You don't—" he sighed, shaking his head. "I don't have a choice. He's never gonna stop."

"What're you planning?" Her words, a whisper.

"One last run. Pull together enough cash to pay him off in exchange for my freedom. Then I'm out. For good."

"You think you can just hang up your tools once

you get a taste of all that cash in your pocket again? Come on, Pete… we both know the temptation of fast money."

"I'm not doing it like that this time." Peter scrubbed roughly at his face. *Aren't I? What am I doing then?* Peter wrestled with his thoughts. A new plan meshing together before his eyes. "I'm gonna buy 'em cheap at the auctions. Flip 'em over and make the cash that way. It won't be as fast, but it'll be legal. I just need to get 'em cheap enough to make it work. Maybe get onto a wrecker's payroll. Scavenge around. Nothing's set yet."

"You're going to need a team."

"No… I won't drag anyone down if this goes to shit. I'll do it myself."

"Pete, you can't drive two cars at once. At the very least, you're going to need a driver to help you drop and deliver."

"I know. I've been working it over in my head. I've got an idea or two. I'll sort it. The first issue I need to sort out is my 'style'. I need it to stand out enough to get over the line, but plain enough to slip under Reece's radar. Any suggestions?"

"Design was always your strength, not mine. But I'm damn good behind the wheel of just about any car you sit me in. Let me help you."

"Beth, no! I won't have you—"

"You know I can do it. You know I'm the best. Who else can you ask, honestly?"

Peter paused. Defeat loomed. She was right, of course. She was one of the best drivers he'd ever known. Instinctual, like himself. But could he do it? Could he knowingly put her in danger? Could he trust her? Tom had made it clear he wouldn't be that kind of help. There wasn't anyone else he trusted with his secret or his vehicles. She'd be an asset, but that meant she'd also be a target. *Hasn't today proved she's already a target?!*

"What do you want out of it?" His words were calloused. The more money she wanted, the more cars he would have to push out to make enough for himself.

"Charming, Pete. A girl offers you her services, and that's all you can say." Her words were laced with innuendo, but Peter wasn't falling for it. She was dodging. His temper flared.

"Answer the question, Liz," was his icy reply. It worked. 'Bee' was a friend. Lost love. A danger to his heart and sense of good reason. Liz, though, Liz was a stranger. A potential business deal in the making. Liz didn't turn his blood to magma.

FIVE

Everything was coming together. Now that Tommy knew Peter was doing it on the up, he'd agreed to help. Be a scout for good buys and help with parts where he could. Peter refused Tommy get any more involved than that.

Peter drove his gloved fists into the weighted bag. *Thump, thump, thump.* He'd organised a paint and panel supplier who—for a fee—would keep the transaction details on the low. *Thump, thump, thump.* The wrecking yard. The decal guy. The bank loan to get him started. *Thump, thump, thump.*

Peter steadied the bag. Sweat ran down his spine as he wiped his forehead on a shirt sleeve. It'd been three days since he'd heard from Elizabeth. Where was she at? Was she having second thoughts? Would she back out last minute? Maybe she'd decided she wanted more than just 'an adrenaline-fuelled distraction.'

Thump, thump, thump.

His muscles burned. How long had he been at this now? Exhausting himself before going into a hell spiral of bad food, no sleep, and over-working wasn't his smartest decision. But it would all be worth it. This had to work.

His phone buzzed on the side table, pulling him back to the present. He ditched his gloves and retrieved it. 'Bee.'

It's sorted. I'm commitment-free and all yours. When do we start?

Peter's head had been spinning off its axis with doubt all week, yet here she was coming through for him. Why did he expect her to bail on him? She'd always had his back. So, what was it?

A tiny voice whispered from the depths of his mind. 'It's all coming too easy.' *Yes! That's it!* For the longest time, Peter's life had been hard. So hard. He'd grown to expect things turning to shit in his hands. It was only a matter of time before his luck skidded to a whiplashing halt, wasn't it? Only time would be the teller of all. Peter texted her the details of their first auction. He'd bought a ute. He couldn't use Tommy's cars to get him around with all the extra kilometres he'd be doing now. It wasn't anything fancy, but the tray would be good for hauling supplies, so it did the job. He agreed to pick her up and they would go together.

Peter trolled through the cars online, checking daily for any late-comers to the auction. After making a shortlist from the website photographs, he and Elizabeth arrived early on auction day to register and go over the contenders for damage or irreparable pitfalls. Any cars they chose needed to be straight if they were to return a decent profit—correcting and respraying damaged panels was expensive and labour intensive.

Two of the three vehicles they found were good enough for Peter, but the third earned itself a 'hard pass' due to hail damage. It was a start. Together, Peter and Elizabeth stood in the back of the gathered buyers. Car after car, they watched people bid and win. Prices varied and Peter worried he wouldn't be able to secure his picks for the price he wanted. If this didn't work, he was screwed.

Finally, the first of his two drove into the crowded warehouse. He shifted his weight from one leg to the other. Nervous energy flowed as the stakes became real. Elizabeth's hand touched his momentarily, drawing his attention to her. She gave him an encouraging smile and returned her gaze to the auctioneer.

Two hours and several signatures later, Peter was the temporary owner of what he hoped were his first two tickets to freedom. *After a tonne of hard work!* Hard work he could do. Getting through it, working so closely with Elizabeth… he wasn't so sure.

The following weeks passed in a haze of late nights, long days, and snatched meals on the run. Peter added a microwave to the workbench relics in the old hangar and learned that a decade's worth of dust was officially enough to kill a stereo. He replaced the old gal with a second-hand boombox of similar vintage to its predecessor.

Microwave meals and protein bars were keeping him alive, just. There were some nights that Peter just didn't want to return to the hangar, but this wasn't one of those nights. He'd finished his second car and the first one had sold without issue. The next three cars wouldn't arrive until the following morning, so tonight was easy. An oil change, replace a wiper blade, a vacuum and wash. An early night and a rest from the more strenuous stuff.

With the car up on ramps, Peter lay beneath it. He unscrewed the sump plug to drain the blackened oil. Feeling for the rag beside his head, he wiped his oily hand intently while humming along to the song playing in the background. He inched out from under the car and startled at a figure standing inside the entry door.

"Jesus, Bee. You scared the shit outta me! Don't sneak up on a guy next time, would ya?"

"Sorry. Seeing you all mechanic-like caught me off guard and I forgot to speak up."

Peter was smiling before he could stop himself. She'd always loved the grease and shed talk as much as she had the fast cars and thrill of the chase. She was every bad boy's dream. Peter closed the door to memory lane.

"I thought we agreed on tomorrow? It won't be ready tonight. Well, not until later anyway." Having her there was unnerving.

"Relax, I just came by to see if you needed any help. I bought you a spiced chicken and salad wrap. Thought you could do with something decent in your system."

Peter toyed with the rag still in his hands. "Thanks. I'm starving actually." Climbing up from the floor, he wiped the seat of his jeans and headed for the workbench where she now hovered. Peter chucked the rag onto the counter and turned the music down.

Noting his dirty hands, Elizabeth opened one end for him so he could hold it without it tasting like his hands smelled.

"Thanks."

"You're very welcome."

Together, the pair stood leaning against the bench. Peter eating and Elizabeth admiring the new vibe he'd given to the car. She always had kind words for his efforts. He reminded himself not to get attached.

"Well, look… thanks for the dinner. It was amazing, but I'd better get back to it. Standing around doesn't bring in the money. I'll see you tomorrow, like we planned?" He didn't want to be rude, but he needed to stay focused on his end goal and whenever Elizabeth was around, everything seemed to blur.

"I've nowhere else I need to be tonight. Put me to work." Elizabeth hoisted herself up to sit on top of the workbench.

Peter spun towards her, an arm outstretched. "Careful! There's shit everywhere up there, you'll get your pants all—" He felt his heart accelerate. Suddenly, it felt as though his dinner was stuck in his throat. No air reaching his lungs. He needed to walk away. Finish the car so he could go home for the night, but his legs refused to comply.

"PJ." Elizabeth's voice was so quiet Peter wondered if he'd imagined it. She laid a hand along his jaw and pulled him to her. When her soft lips touched his, Peter's eyes drifted closed. Elizabeth nipped at his lower lip, inviting him to deepen the kiss. Heat and arousal licked along his spine. *God, she tastes good. Sweet. Even better than I remember.* Desire overwhelmed him. He needed to feel her. All of her.

Peter centred himself between her thighs and pulled her close. A combination of memory and reality merged in Peter's mind as Elizabeth wrapped her arms and legs around him like her survival depended on it. *Holy shit, I've missed her! Missed this. How she feels pressed against me. The urgency she always expresses. The one that makes me feel like I'm the only man alive! The only one who can give her exactly what she needs.* He felt her fiery core against his stomach, short-circuiting his brain.

Removing his hands from her hips, Peter dropped them to the workbench on either side of her and broke the kiss. He leaned back, angling for distance to think, but with her legs tightly around him, he couldn't escape. Resting his forehead on her shoulder, he closed his eyes and took a fortifying breath. His erection, painful in the confines of his jeans.

"What is it, PJ?" Elizabeth mirrored his pose, resting her forehead on his opposite shoulder.

Together they breathed. Peter remained silent, needing more time to get his thoughts under control. *She is too tempting.*

"Pete—"

"I'm sorry. I can't do this. You should go." Peter reached around behind his shoulders and untangled himself from within her arms. He was grateful she didn't fight him and unwound her legs, freeing him from her spell and the allure of her body. He couldn't allow her any deeper into his life than he already had. Too many people were trying to kill him and her time here was temporary. Peter knew his heart wouldn't survive losing her again.

"Pete, I'm sorry. Let me help."

"I don't think that's a good idea."

"I don't want to go. Please… at least let me give you a hand with the car. I promise… strictly work. Does it need a vacuum? I could do that while you're finishing up the messy stuff. You don't want to get anything on the interior, and you've already got grease on your jeans. So…"

Peter deliberated. *I'm going to regret this.*

"Ok… but just work. Nothing else. I… I can't offer you anything else, Beth."

Peter saw sadness in her eyes when he turned to her, but she hid it quickly behind an over-enthusiastic smile and raised her hand with three fingers skyward. "Scouts honour."

With the two of them working together, it hadn't taken long to get the car completely ready for the coming day's departure. Peter was careful to keep his distance, but snuck glimpses of her when she wasn't looking. She had reignited the fire in him that he had long ago thought, dead.

Elizabeth wound up the extension lead and was packing up the industrial vacuum. Peter was cleaning up a couple of last items on the workbench before heading for the stereo.

"Leave it a sec, please. I love this song."

"I'm surprised you remember it," Peter replied, immediately cursing himself mentally for admitting he too remembered it. When he looked at her, she was blushing.

"Why wouldn't I?" she challenged.

"Nothing. I just... nothing." Peter swallowed the lump in his throat. How many times tonight would he have to fight off the feelings and memories that she was evoking in him? Peter wasn't sure how much more he could take. Having her here, the song playing, them fooling around earlier tonight... it was all déjà vu. Peter tried to extinguish the ancient memories bubbling to the surface. They came through faster and stronger than he could control. He was an idiot who needed to get a handle on himself. He was a grown-arse man who was letting his head and his dick mess with his priorities.

"It was the song playing the day you and I... You know. Here." She all but whispered.

Elizabeth could've punched him. He felt like she had. *She remembers.* The electricity zinging between them earlier was back and it was palpable. Their relationship was a tricky thing. A powerful thing. Drawn to her like the compass needle points north. He could try to fight it for as long as he wanted, but Elizabeth—like the natural magnetic field of Mother Earth—would always win in the end. He and Elizabeth were both older. Both old enough to have learned some self-control and definitely old enough to know it wouldn't end well, but none of that mattered. In that moment, under the influence of the music's sorcery, they were two souls chasing unity, ridding each other of their clothes with possessive hands.

SIX

Other than the auctions themselves, transporting cars and that one carnal night at the hangar, Peter and Elizabeth didn't spend too much time together in the days and weeks that followed. Peter had gently reminded her he couldn't afford distractions. He needed her as a driver so she should fill in her spare time visiting her mum—while she still could. To his relief, Elizabeth did just that.

One Thursday night at the shop, Peter was working late to repay the hours he'd missed through the day in pursuit of more auction cars. Tommy said he needed to catch up on paperwork, so agreed to hang around with him. Tommy went up the road to buy them both some dinner.

Peter lay on a mechanics trolley beneath a car

bonnet when he heard footsteps nearing. "I've got one more bolt. I'll just get this one in, so it's all done." Peter announced, knowing Tommy would haul him out otherwise. Something sounded from beside the car Peter worked beneath. Without warning, he was jerked out from his greasy nook. The bright workshop lights burned his eyes before a bulky shadow moved above him. Before Peter could recognise what he was looking at, something hard connected with his chest. A grunt escaped Peter before he sucked in a ragged breath that felt like a thousand knives stabbing him from the inside out.

Peter clutched his ribs, convinced he would split in two if he let go. He rolled to his side, falling from the trolley, sending it skating backwards. His attacker dropped the weapon to the floor with a metallic clatter that exploded in Peter's ears. Still cradling his rib cage, Peter curled up into a ball and rocked side to side, trying to ease the pain. Everything went black.

"Pete? Pete, wake up! What happened, man?" Peter woke. Someone was shouting at him. He was shaking. He wished he could stop. Every movement felt like something inside his chest cavity was shattering. The yelling got louder and Peter realised it was Tom.

"Tommy?"

"I'm here. What happened?"

"I… I don't know. I was… working." Peter tried to remember, but everything was foggy. Everything hurt. His head. His chest. The pain of it all, making his stomach recoil. He needed to sit up. Pushing himself up from the concrete floor, fresh pain ripped through him. Bile rose and before he could stop himself, he vomited. Peter's memory began righting itself. He was in the workshop. He'd been just about finished when someone hit him. Footsteps… they had run off. He scanned the floor. For what? The breaker bar glinted at him under the fluorescent lights. "That." He pointed weakly. "They hit me with that. Across the ribs. Think they're broken." Peter managed before another round of nausea erupted from him. He wished he'd stop vomiting. Every time he did, he learned a new lesson in pain.

"Jesus! Did you get a look at 'im?"

Peter shook his head no. Relieved when this action didn't evoke more pain.

Peter noted the worry lines creasing Tom's forehead as he nodded in silent agreement with what Peter already knew to be true. They were broken. He needed to go to the hospital and make sure there weren't any splinters or punctured organs.

The waiting room was quiet and it wasn't long before Peter's name was called. Standing hurt and sent another wave of nausea through him. Tom caught and steadied him.

"You ok? You want me to come in with ya?"

"Would you? If they poke around my ribs, I'm gonna pass out and that'll make it hard to answer their questions."

Worry lines etched Tom's face. Peter guessed that he himself must look a mess to cause such concern in Tom. His suspicions were confirmed when he walked past a pane of glass, throwing his reflection back at him like a mirror. He hardly recognised the grey face and hunched figure looking back at him. He moved to straighten but winced and resumed his 'old man shuffle' to sit on the Emergency Department gurney.

A man dressed in scrubs entered the cubicle. A doctor? Nurse? Peter couldn't tell. He didn't care. He just wanted the pain to stop. *Please let this guy be capable of shipping me off to a med-induced paradise! Preferably until everything is healed weeks from now. I have too much shit to do.*

After countless medical personnel had probed his ribs, x-rays taken and several curse words spoken, Peter was discharged into Tom's care with a sweet concoction of god-only-knows what running through his veins.

Tom wrestled a drunk-like Peter, humming and dancing without a care towards the hospital carpark. "Pete, watch what you're doin'. And quit dancing around. You heard what the doc said! Right, watch your head. Ok... now, sit still!" Tom shook his head as he circled the car and climbed in behind the wheel.

Peter woke, groggy and confused. The sunlight was too bright. It hurt his eyes. Noises became clear. Someone was stirring something.

Where am I? Why am I hungover? Don't tell me I caved after all these years? Going cold turkey wasn't easy, but what made me cave after all this time? Yep, mouth feels like I've been eating sand... if ever there was a sure sign... this was it. Shit!

"Mornin', cupcake. How're you feeling?"

Peter opened his eyes and found Tom's face peering upside down at him from behind the couch, coffee cup in hand. *Tom got me wasted? After everything I've been through.* Anger shot through him and he moved to get up. Pain seared through his side, forcing him back down as air hissed through his gritted teeth. Tom now stood squarely in front of him, all signs of teasing gone.

"What the fuck, Tommy?" Peter looked around

the room for answers. His confusion heightened now.

"You were attacked. Last night at the shop. You've got four broken ribs on your left side and deep tissue bruising up the wazoo. Hospital? X-rays? Do you not remember any of this?"

Flashes of the previous night came into focus as Peter recalled the attack. "The breaker bar. I remember. What the hell did they give me at the hospital? I feel like I've been on the bottle." Peter slowly raised his good arm to scrub at his face. He felt dirty and sleep-eyed.

An uneasy tension loomed over Peter. He had question marks about the previous night, despite being completely alert now. Pieces were missing and he didn't like it. He'd suffered plenty of injuries in his time, but never broken ribs. Peter guessed they took about as long to heal as any other bone. If that were true, then he was *not* going to be a happy man. He didn't have time to be laid up. He had work to do.

"Everything's pretty hazy. What's the verdict?" Peter saw Tom hesitate. "Give it to me straight. I already know I ain't gonna' like it." Peter scowled at the ceiling to emphasise his point.

"Six weeks is the norm. Your level of bruising could hinder that process. But if you follow doc's orders to take it easy and do the breathing exercises they gave you, you should heal without complications."

"Breathing exercises! Do I look like some yoga tosser to you?!" Peter exploded, earning himself a fresh round of agony.

"I didn't make the rules, man. I'm just relaying what they told you. For the record though…That's exactly what you told them last night, too."

"Shit! What the hell am I gonna do now?! Can't work. Can't finish the cars I've got. Fuck!" Still in his uniform from the previous night, Peter suddenly longed for a shower. Would he even be able to do that? Or dress and undress himself? Asking for help wasn't his thing. He wasn't good at it and he didn't like how weak it made him feel.

"It happened at the shop so I can organise worker's comp if you want to take that angle."

"You and I both know it had nothing to do with the shop. I'll cop it. There's no way I'm letting you take any more hits on my sorry-arse's behalf. I don't even know what to say. Christ! I'm so sorry, Tommy. You'd be better off letting me go. Ball and chain 'round your bloody neck, I am." Peter finger-combed his disheveled hair roughly.

"Yeah… but life'd be boring. C'mon. Let's get you up and I'll drive you home to get some clothes.

I think you'd better come and stay with me for a few. Need your steak cut up for ya and all that. I draw the line though at wiping' your hairy arse. I don't care how you manage that, but I'll have no part in it. Comprende?"

The two men chuckled. Peter winced and offered Tom a gently sculpted salute. He had no words for how much he loved this man. Peter had dragged Tommy through hell and back, and the guy never even flinched. Peter owed him everything.

At his house, collecting up what he would need for an indefinite stay at Tommy's house, Peter's body protested all the movement and blood that was suddenly being forced around his veins. How could one sharp hit make his body ache in areas seemingly unrelated to his ribs? Why did his neck hurt? And his arm? His head pounded, adding its two cents to the cause.

Peter's phone rang from the other room. He couldn't get to it in time unless he moved fast and that would increase the throbbing. He ignored it.

Tom leaned against the bedroom door. "It's Beth. Want me to answer it?"

Fuck! They'd discussed the idea of working together up at the hangar over the weekend. *Fuck!* "Let it go to message. I'll call her later." Tom bided Peter's wishes and returned to the lounge room, phone in hand.

Back at Tom's house, Peter enjoyed the heat of a shower while it fogged up the screen. He'd had to all but cut himself out of his work polo and wasn't sure how he would get his clean t-shirt on, but Peter refused to think about that before it was necessary. From his shorts pocket on the bathroom floor, Peter heard his phone ring. It was probably Bee... again! He couldn't avoid her forever. What was he going to tell her? He didn't have any answers yet himself. He ducked under the stream of water, drowning out the sound.

Peter returned to the lounge room, his stomach roiling with nausea. He'd overdone it. *You just need to sit for a minute.*

"You look like shit, man. You need to take something for the pain. Want me to get you the Oxycodone?"

"I'll survive." Peter shook his head.

"You don't need to be the hero. I've had a broken rib, it's the worse pain imaginable. A couple of days on the harder stuff won't unravel you. You're stronger these days."

"I'll live! I don't want any pills."

Tom threw his hands into the air. "Your funeral."

Tom stalked off to the kitchen. "I've got to head

to the shop and make sure everything's still running. You know where everything is. Call me if you get stuck. Lauren'll be home in about halfa'. She knows you're staying here, so don't panic. Back in a bit."

Peter heard the front door close followed by the grunt of eight cylinders firing up outside. He closed his eyes and laid his head back against the couch. Ouch! Unable to get comfortable or find a position that didn't cause him agony, Peter relented and took half the prescribed dose of the powerful painkiller. He wouldn't use anymore, he just needed to get some sleep.

Bee's hand was sliding into his pants when Peter jolted awake. He immediately winced, finding himself alone in the house. His hard-on throbbed almost as painfully as his ribs. With a muttered curse, he adjusted himself one-armed and awkward, on the couch. *Damn opioids! Shoulda known they'd screw with my head!*

From the kitchen, Peter heard the faint jingle of keys. Lauren was home. Peter thanked the devil that she hadn't arrived five minutes earlier or she'd have seen his pistol and that'd just be weird! Carefully, he sat up on the couch.

"Shit. Sorry, Pete. I didn't mean to wake you."

"All good, Lolly. It's your house. Don't tip-toe

around on my account. I'm enough of a burden as it is. Hey. Thanks for letting me stay here by the way. It's really kind of you. I know Tom doesn't mind, but you hardly needed another foul-mouthed, bad-habited louse on your plate. Or your couch. No hard feelings if you want me to clear out…and it can just be between us if you're worried about Tommy. I get it. I'll just tell him I need my own bed or something." Peter sat up awkwardly.

"Don't be ridiculous, Pete. You're family. Stay as long as you need to. You're no bother to either of us and I'll not have you telling yourself otherwise, you hear? Now… don't mind me. I'm only here for a quick change of clothes and then I'm going for a run before Tommy gets home. Any requests for tea? I was thinking tacos but I could be persuaded into nachos instead… if that rises your rebel?" she said, trekking down towards her and Tom's bedroom.

Peter chuckled and immediately regretted it. "Nachos need two hands. Tacos… I can probably manage on my own with some help to make them." He called after her, awkwardly.

"Tacos it is then. I'll grab some soft-shells while I'm gone, which should be easier for you to get through. Back soon." She returned, whisking her hair up into a scruffy top-knot as she passed.

Peter smiled, watching her bounce out the door

in her tights and baggy shirt. Tom was one lucky brother.

Peter needed to move. He'd been lying on the couch most of the day and his whole body felt stiff. He stood carefully and was about to move when vigorous knocking sounded at the front door. Peter smiled, wondering what she'd forgotten.

"What'd you for—" Peter's words fell away at the sight of a fiery-eyed, wild-looking Elizabeth. *Shit!* "How'd you—"

"You could've answered your damn phone, Pete! I've been worried stupid!"

"Why?" Peter shook his head in confusion. "How'd you know I was here?"

"How do you think? I went to the shop when you wouldn't answer. Tommy said you'd had an accident or something. Are you ok? What happened—"

"Why were you so worried? I don't understand."

"Why?! Have you forgotten that *I* was chased through the streets two months ago by your nemesis and we've been dodging him and his disciples ever since while you try to make cash on the side? Something that we both know Reece wouldn't think kindly of if he knew, so I think it's justified that when you suddenly stopped answering your phone that maybe the worst has happened. Why didn't you pick up the phone or call me—"

"Bee… take a breath, babe," the word was out of his mouth before he could take it back. "I'll explain. I'm ok. Please, breathe."

Elizabeth was against him in a single step. Her lips melded with his in desperation and worry. Taken by surprise, Peter didn't have time to refuse her or see sense. Her tongue invaded his mouth, short-circuiting his brain, and he reciprocated mindlessly. She tasted of peppermint. Peter's body sprang to attention after his earlier dream, reminding him that this was a bad idea. He broke off the kiss, wincing when he angled back too sharply. Elizabeth released his hip, concerned.

"Wasn't you." He shook his head. "I gotta remember to stop moving so suddenly."

Elizabeth stared worriedly at him. Knowing he had stirred all this emotion in her, both warmed and unsettled Peter.

"Pete, I'm—"

"Don't worry about it." He stepped out of her arms. Out of temptation's reach.

Leaving the door open for her to enter, Peter went to the dining table, where he folded himself into a chair cautiously.

"So… what happened?" She wouldn't let this go.

"I was at work. Tommy'd gone to get us some

dinner when someone busted me in half with the breaker bar. Left me with a few broken ribs."

Elizabeth inched closer. She leaned to touch his thigh as she sat on the adjacent chair.

"I'm fine, Beth. I'll live." Her hand froze between them. Peter fought the urge to let her comfort him. He couldn't do this. "I have to work out what I'm going to do. How I'm gonna get the other cars finished. God knows how long I'll be out for and you'll be heading back to the city as I'm coming good. I don't see how I can make it all work, but I'll cover your costs somehow. I just need a little time to figure things out."

"Pete. That's not—"

"No. I will."

"Damn it, Pete! That's not why I'm helping you! I don't want your money. I feel responsible! You have been taking abuse from these thugs all because of me—"

"It wasn't you, though, was it? We both know it wasn't you because that was the same day I saw—"

"Agh! You're infuriating, you know that? Being around you makes me feel alive! I didn't even know I missed it until I showed up back here and got chased. And then your smooth-as-silk voice came through the car speakers. You know, I realised later that I wasn't even scared during the chase. I loved it.

All of it."

"This was a bad idea. I knew I should never—"

"Pete, wait. I know you don't like asking. You think it makes you weak and vulnerable. You think you're going to corrupt me, but I'm not a kid anymore. Please let me help you. You can be the brain and I'll be the hands. Together, we can still do this. What do you say?" All business-like except the smirk tugging at her lip, Elizabeth held out her hand. Peter stared at it a minute before taking it in his good one. He shook it gently. *This is going to end in tears. Her tears. Strictly business, Jones, and stick to the plan!*

"I can't drive so…"

"When should I pick you up? Tomorrow? Since I assume you're no longer working at the shop currently?"

"Actually, I'm gonna do a few days as the office bitch, but not tomorrow. So yes. Eight AM too early for you?"

"Perfect. I'll be here." Elizabeth stood from her seat. "Oh, and Pete… try to get some sleep. You look awful." Peter rolled his eyes. *If only it was that simple!*

SEVEN

Having Elizabeth back in the hangar alongside him was an odd feeling. At first, Peter was conscious of her every movement. A distraction that pulled his attention away from his work.

As days passed, Elizabeth familiarised herself with the tools while Peter guided her and explained what needed to go where. No longer jumpy with her in his space, Peter admitted to himself that it was actually nice to have company, especially in the evenings when they would work quietly, humming along to the radio.

The idea of 'sponging off his friends' sat poorly with Peter, so after a week, he moved back home. His only concession was allowing Lauren to send him home with several pre-packed meals she'd started freezing for this very purpose. She knew him well... knew he'd never stay long enough to heal properly. She truly was an angel.

It felt fantastic to be back in his own place, using his own shower and sleeping in his own bed. Elizabeth, staying with her mother as she was, also worked well for Peter because it required her to drive straight past his door on her way home. She insisted on dropping him off and picking him up each evening.

Back in his ripped jeans, ready for another night of grease and spanners, Peter waited for the familiar text saying that she was outside. A knock sounded on the front door. Peter rolled his eyes. *She drank too much tea with her mum again and now she needs a leak.* "You've really got to stop—" Peter swung the door open wide, ready for her to bolt past him when he met the steely gaze of Reece and froze. The two men faced off for a second.

"Couldn't find any more minions to do your dirty work, hey Reece?" Fear and dread knotted in Peter's gut. "What'll it be this time? You gonna bust a few more ribs? Have your thugs pin me down while you kick the shit outta me again? Haven't done that one for a while now. Huh?" Peter was surprised how confident he sounded. He knew what Reece was capable of.

As if to highlight his thoughts, Peter saw a flicker of light reflect off something in Reece's hand. A knife. As if in slow motion, Peter saw surprise register in Reece's eyes at the same time that dread must have filled his own. Footsteps. *Elizabeth!*

"Run, Bee! He's—"

"Elizabeth Mason, what a—" Both men spoke at the same time.

"Reece Jones... how is it possible that you have grown even more deplorable after all these years?" Elizabeth challenged their childhood nemesis. Peter grimaced.

"Beth, don't! He has a knife. Get outta here!"

"For once, sweet lips... you should probably listen to your boyfriend. While I'm feeling generous enough to let you *walk* away," Reece said cooly, rotating the knife between his fingertips.

"Go, Beth. Please." Peter pleaded.

"I think I'll take my chances you under-achieving, over-compensating parasite," she directed at Reece, ignoring Peter's plea's.

"Beth, have you lost your mind? Just go already!" Peter strained.

"I'm not leaving, PJ. It's time we settle this. All of it."

Using the private nickname as she did now in front of Reece, Peter's stomach turned to jelly. She'd never called him PJ in front of anybody, always reserving it for only his ears. Peter saw how it hit Reece like a fist in the gut. She was playing a dangerous game and she didn't know how unstable Reece had become in the years since she'd left. He needed to get her out of here before Reece did something none of them could take back. *I will NOT let him hurt her! He can kill me, but I need to get her away from here!*

"Reece. I will meet you. Anywhere you say. You can kill me. I know it's what you want. Just… not here. Don't hurt—"

"There is no way I'm letting you boys fight this out without me. This shit started with me. It's damn well gonna end with me."

"Beth, this isn't about—"

"Isn't it? Are you sure about that, Pete? This whole rivalry thing seemed to gear up right around the same time Reece caught us fooling around in the hangar…like…a bazillion years ago! And you…" Elizabeth pointed a sleek index finger at Reece's nose. "Seemed to develop a deathly vendetta against Pete here, scarcely more than a day after you cornered me between the parked cars, forced yourself onto me and I told you that you could do what you wanted to my body but you would never get near my heart or mind. That I loved PJ, and nothing you could do was ever going to change that. Despite everything you did…you didn't scare me then and you definitely don't scare me now. Crawl back under the shitty rock you came from and rot, you perverted fuck! I kept your secrets to protect PJ, but knowing it went down this way, I wish I'd spoken up years ago."

The world stopped while Peter took in Elizabeth's words. She hadn't been with Reece by choice. He'd forced her. That day. Between the cars. He'd been such an idiot! All these years, he'd thought she'd betrayed their love. That he wasn't worthy of her.

The three of them faced off before chaos erupted. Reece swung at Elizabeth with enough force to lift her off the ground and dump her on her backside. Peter lunged at Reece, grabbing the arm that held the knife. The two men grappled until Peter felt the knife slice through the flesh at his shoulder. He yelled out in pain as he heard the knife clatter to the floor while Reece continued to come at him. Reece's fists connected with him once, twice, then a third blow came to his ribs, and he felt them break all over again. The pain was too much. Peter felt himself slipping into a heavy fog, but he fought against it. *I need to keep her safe. He'll kill her.*

He struggled to find his feet. Tried to keep his

eyes open. He couldn't tell which way was up. It felt like he was being thrown around by waves, unable to find the surface.

He heard yelling somewhere nearby, but couldn't make his brain decipher what was going on. He suddenly couldn't remember where he was or why he needed to fight. The answers were just beyond reach, but something told him it was important, whatever it was.

Peter drifted in and out of consciousness. Voices murmured and his body was being tugged this way and that. He frowned. There were several people talking. Some further away than others. A man and a woman were talking close by. They seemed to speak in some type of foreign language. BP, tachycardic, laceration. These words felt like they should mean something to Peter, but in his disconnected state, he couldn't find the links in his brain to meld everything together. Frustrated, he turned his focus to the discussion happening further away. Men were talking—two, maybe three? Something about a suspect and no forced entry. None of the words made any sense to Peter, but something told him they should. Something continued to poke at his conscious that he knew the answers, but he couldn't retrieve them.

The voices closest to him grew loud. They told

him to 'hold still'. 'He was safe.' Words had found their meanings in his mind. They made sense again. He fought. He couldn't find his voice, but he wasn't safe. Someone thought he'd committed a crime. Had he? The last thing he remembered was leaving the shop with Tommy.

His body felt pinned and he couldn't move his legs. With a clenched fist, he swung to dislodge whoever was holding him captive, but pain ripped through his torso and shoulder, causing him to gasp and drop the arm automatically. Finally, his eyes decided to join the battle and he squinted against the light. Silhouettes moved closely above him, obviously the thugs containing him. He remembered. He was at home. Reece…a knife. *Shit, Elizabeth! Where is she?* He screamed out for her in a panic. *If he's hurt her… I will extract that son of a bitch's eyeballs from his sockets with a shifter, so help me god!*

"Where is she? What have you animals done with—"

"I'm here, PJ. I'm right here." Elizabeth's voice was calm. He didn't know where she'd come from, but she sat beside his head, stroking the hair back from his forehead. "It's ok. Let the ambos' do their job."

"Reece! And, and… Reece is—"

"Pete, look at me. It's ok. I'll explain everything later. Stop fighting them so they can help you. Please."

Peter felt his muscles relax and his fear subside as Elizabeth continued her soft strokes. There was no fear or worry in her voice. He could trust her. He was so tired. Peter let his eyes drift closed. *I'll just rest for a minute.* As they slid shut, he remembered her word 'ambo'.

"Bee?"

"I'm still here."

"No drugs. Don't let them give me drugs. I'm clean. I stopped everything…when you left. I'm not… not that guy now. No drugs. Don't let—"

"It's ok, babe…I know. Shh."

Peter thought she sounded sad. Like she might have even been crying, but he couldn't come back from the deep fog to check.

EIGHT

Peter woke to an annoying beeping sound. Whatever it was... he would pay good money for someone to shut it up. His whole body felt stiff and yet oddly numb. He tried to swallow but found no saliva. His lips stuck to his teeth. He was so thirsty. What time was it? Peter opened his eyes and found a slumped Elizabeth sitting in a chair with her head resting on the bed beside his hip. Her face was relaxed, and her mouth had popped open sometime since she'd fallen asleep. He was in the hospital? The beeping came from a machine dripping some sort of clear liquid into him through a tube attached to his hand. The bag was almost empty. Peter felt his blood pressure rising. He'd been in hospitals enough to know that doctors fed drugs through IVs.

He reached for the cannula connected to his hand, only to be struck with instant pain. Cold sweat broke out across his body. He winced, drawing air through clenched teeth. *God damn it!*

Elizabeth woke at the commotion and stood automatically. She took his hand, careful not to dislodge the tubes. Without a word, she brushed his hair away from his face. Peter jerked away from her touch, earning himself another lashing of the relentless pain.

"Shh, shh… you'll reopen your shoulder… or your chest."

"I told you… no drugs!" Peter hissed, looking pointedly at the bag hanging from the IV pole above his head.

"Huh. Oh… no, no. Listen to me. That is just fluids and antibiotics to make sure you don't get an infection. This here… this is for your pain—the only meds you could get addicted to—and they're managed by you. See? You can press the button to release it. But it won't let you over-do it. Please stop trying to pull out your drip. I swear to you. There's nothing addictive in there."

"Where's Reece? Does he know where I am?"

"Reece won't be bothering you. Please try to relax. You're going to hurt yourself more." Elizabeth averted her eyes, but Peter saw the tear on her cheek. He swiped at it with his good hand. "I was so scared, PJ. I really thought you might not wake up. There was so much blood and you were lying there and—"

"Hey…" Peter clutched her hand gently in his. "I'm so sorry you saw me like that. I didn't want you anywhere near the danger, but you arrived before I could get a message to you. Did Reece take off? You need to be careful, Bee. He won't stop. He'll come aft—"

"Reece won't be coming after anyone. PJ… Reece is dead. I didn't plan to kill him. I was only trying to stop him. But I accidentally hit an artery and he bled out. He was gone in a few minutes, maybe less. There was nothing I could do. I'm sorry, Pete. I know you were rivals, but he was still your brother."

"He stopped being my brother years ago. And make no mistake, he was there to kill me, so he obviously didn't—" Peter couldn't say the words. "Thank you… for saving my life." Peter's jaw flexed. The depth of their rivalry ran bone-deep. "Beth… is it true? What you said about Reece? That he… the day I saw you two between the cars. That he… forced you?" Peter watched hurt and confusion mar her beautiful face.

"You were there? You saw us?"

"There was no struggle. I saw that."

"He said he'd kill you… that you'd be dead by sundown if I fought or told a soul. He was crazy. I couldn't risk it. So, I closed my eyes and heart, but I was never the same." Elizabeth trailed off, wiping a tear.

"I wish you'd've told me. I would've hunted him down and ripped his throat out."

"After that, I couldn't face you. I felt violated but somehow guilty that I hadn't tried to stop him. Like I must've loved you less because I hadn't tried." Elizabeth stared, her thoughts far away. "These days I'd do everything differently but—" She shrugged. "I can't change the past. So instead… I moved away. I started making smarter choices and learned Jujitsu. I had a lot of anger, so I channeled it into learning how to take someone like him down in case I ever needed to again. He was only supposed to be incapacitated, not killed."

"Better this way, if you ask me. I'm sorry… that I didn't protect you. I never even thought that he might've blackmailed you."

"Wait… you thought… you thought he and I were? Oh god! Have you honestly been walking around for the last seven years thinking I carried a torch for Reece?"

It was Peter's turn to stare at the bedsheets. He

tried to process Elizabeth's words and how different things might have been if he'd known all along. She'd always been drawn to the wrong things in life. Dangerous things. They lit a fire in her and damn, it looked hot on her! The pin-up of 'bad girls are sexy'.

Peter laid his head back and closed his eyes. His jaw clenched and unclenched as he reminded himself of all the reasons why he needed to leave Beth alone. She was bad for him. She held a power over him like he'd never experienced before or since. One click of her slender fingers and he'd do her every bidding. And him… wasn't he bad for her? Definitely! She had a life. A successful job and people who respected her. She needed to stay as far away from him as this earth made possible!

"I know what you're doing, Pete. Don't."

Peter felt the bed move, but couldn't open his eyes and make her leave. Not yet.

"Don't." Elizabeth cupped his face gently, sending goosebumps prickling along his skin. The thick lump of emotion in his throat threatened to suffocate him and stubbornly refused to be swallowed down. He leaned into her soft touch and allowed himself to feel. He was an addict again, only this time it wasn't booze or drugs. This addiction was far worse! He craved it. He couldn't deny it.

He'd do anything for it. Which was exactly why he had to stop it. NOW!

A single tear snuck beyond the confines of his closed lids and hung at an outer corner. He willed it to dry and go undetected. Elizabeth's touch was his weakness, but to keep her here was selfish. His attempts to clear his throat remained futile.

"We can't do this," he barely breathed the words. Eyes closed, he knew his resolve—what little of it he had left—would break if he looked at her.

"Pete, stop. There's nothing for me to go back—"

"I can't do this, Bee. Please... just go."

"You listen to me...I'm not going anywhere. I know you feel the same way. I know you better than anyone, and I know what you're doing. Well... not this time. I won't let you do this to us. You're scared and you're pushing me away, just like you always do."

"This isn't about me. Please, Bee." Peter's jaw worked as he tried desperately to keep his emotions under lock. He needed her to go. His heart was breaking and the longer he dragged it out, the more pieces fractured. He knew he was hurting her, but this was for the best. It was for her.

"Look at me." Elizabeth drew him close. Their faces almost touching. Her perfume filled his nostrils. He shook his head, unable to form the words without breaking down. "Look at me, PJ." Two traitor tears leaked from his still closed lids, before being swept away by Elizabeth's soft thumbs. "Please," she breathed.

Peter swallowed again, and this time opened his eyes to see a matching pair of pools perched heavily on Elizabeth's lower lid's. The sight of her like this was the final snap his heart could endure before he would surely die.

"I love you." Elizabeth's chin quivered as she whispered the words and two fresh tears plopped onto Peter's hospital-issued gown.

"You can't love me, Bee. I'm not good for you." He shook his head for emphasis and to remind himself as well.

Elizabeth rested her hand against his heart, careful not to hurt his injuries. "What do you *feel*?"

As the warmth of her touch seeped through the blue cotton, Peter realised he would accept the pain of his battered body a hundred times over if only he could quell the pain in his heart at the thought of losing her again.

"I feel… like my head's going to explode. You don't fight fair." Peter closed his eyes again. Seeing her this way was unbearable.

So close that he felt her breath against his ear, she whispered. "A boy I grew up with once told me 'fighting fair is for sissies', and I've never been a sissy."

Before he could protest, she kissed him. An unleashing of passion and tenderness that sent blood and lust surging through his veins and ravaging every corner of his being.

Incapable of fending her off for a single second longer, Peter met her passion and their tongues collided in a greedy reunion. Would they plummet or would they fly? Peter couldn't be sure. He only knew that the longing in his heart began healing when he let this beautiful woman back into his life... into his soul. He needed her. God, he wanted her. It was finally their time.

NINE

Twelve months later

Peter stood in front of the bathroom mirror, trying to tame the stubborn curl sticking out above his ear. He needed a haircut, but work was so busy these days that leaving early wasn't an option.

He was still cursing at it when Elizabeth entered. His hands stilled as he took in her tanned skin. Her powder blue panties matching their skimpy lace counterpart, barely covering her breasts. Peter's cock twitched. *Fuck, she's hot! She's incredible. So much more than she realises. More than I deserve.*

Thoughts of pinning her against the bathroom door, her legs wrapped around his waist, rushed through his mind.

"What?" she interrupted his daydream.

"Huh? Oh, nothing."

"I know that look. You've got something rolling around in that beautiful mind of yours. What is it?"

"If you think I can concentrate on anything while you're waltzing around my house in skimpy underwear, you don't know me very well." Peter's eyes followed her in the mirror.

"Oh? You like?" She quirked a seductive eyebrow at him.

"Mm, want me to show you how much I *like*? We could blow off this party and go back to bed." Images of her laying beneath him sprung to mind. Ripping the delicate lace off her skin. Unwrapping her like a present on Christmas morning. His erection pounded inside his underwear. And what a delicious present lay beneath. Peter knew how responsive she was to his words alone. She would be so warm, wet, and ready beneath that lace.

"We are *not* missing Lauren's birthday! Get dressed."

Despite her chastising tone, Peter knew there was no weight behind it. Elizabeth was as sex crazy as him. Back before his injuries had healed, she'd taken care of all his *needs*. Over and over again. *Damn you, Lauren.*

At Tommy and Lauren's new house, the place was a hive of friendly chaos and noise. A round-bellied and waddling Lauren greeted them with a hug and kiss on the cheek each. "I'm so glad you guys are here! Thanks for coming."

"You know we wouldn't be anywhere else. Why aren't you sitting down with your feet up and people bringing you food, girl?" Elizabeth assessed Lauren's bulge affectionately. Peter and Lauren shared warm smiles before he shrugged at her in mock apology for his girlfriend's candour.

"Oh please, not you, too." Lauren waved her hand at Elizabeth as if she were a pesky insect. "Honestly, it's too uncomfortable to sit down and too hard to get back up. Even if my feet are the size of watermelons! This little guy has definitely got his daddy's lead foot. Straight into my bladder or ribs usually," Lauren chuckled and rubbed her belly proudly.

"Where's my girl?" Tommy appeared from the kitchen. "Ah, there you are! I've been looking for you everywhere." Peter watched as Tommy wrapped his arms around Lauren and rested his chin on her shoulder to greet them. "Hi guys. Head out the back—we're all out there. Your mum and Johnno are here already, too. Oh, and *please* take her with you. Tie her to a chair if you must! Sit, woman!" Tommy kissed his girlfriend's temple while turning her towards the back door.

Peter watched as Elizabeth took Lauren's arm and steered her towards her own party. Elizabeth, chatting away and Lauren shaking her head with laughter.

"I swear, that woman of mine is driving me crazy. Can you believe she's rearranged the nursery three times this week? Just this week! And don't even get me started on the trouble I'm in if I forget to put my socks in the dirty clothes basket."

Peter laughed fondly as Tommy shook his head. A part of Peter was genuinely scared for his friend. Lauren could be a terrifying force of nature when she wanted to. But the truth was, Peter loved Lauren like a little sister. What she lacked in height, she made up for in spirit. She was spunky and took no shit from no-one. She pushed Tommy to be the best he could be. Challenged him to do better, but was also soft enough to wrap him in her love when the world got tough.

Not many people knew about Tommy's past or the scars that haunted him still, but Peter had grown up with him. Peter and Lauren had formed their own friendship when they'd been thrown together to help save their friend. She was perfect for Tommy.

Pulling himself from the memories, Peter clapped his friend on the back and encouraged him back to the party.

Outside, Peter sat contently, taking it all in. He listened to the conversations being held around him. Witnessed the joy and relief in his mother's eyes and smile as she chatted lovingly with Johnno about his new job. Knowing she was finally safe after all these years. That they all were. The warmth of the afternoon sun heated his shoulders and neck.

After Reece's death, Johnno recounted how Reece had blackmailed him. Peter and his mum accepted him back into their lives easily. They both knew the despicable ways Reece used anyone he could.

Peter's eyes never drifted far from Elizabeth. He was so in love with her, it scared him. It always had. Since before he could remember, she'd been driving him crazy. Throwing seed pods at him. Making mud pies in her mother's garden and blaming him when they'd gotten caught destroying the flowers. The night they'd gotten stoned on her mum's front step, she'd erupted with laughter and woken both their mums up. The next night, when they were both grounded, she'd snuck out to apologise to him. That was the night she'd kissed him.

Until that moment, he'd never looked at her as anything but a mate. She'd always been 'one of the guys.' That was the night everything shifted. The softness of her lips against his. The sweet smell of her mother's homemade soap. He'd laid in his bed for hours that night, wondering how he'd been so blind before that day. Her curves. Her smile.

The two of them were inseparable after that. Where *she* was, he was. They'd done everything together, including getting themselves into hot water with the law. The day Elizabeth's mother shipped her off to live with her aunty in the city, Peter thought someone had ripped his airways out. He wasn't sure he'd ever be able to breathe again.

When he never heard back from her, he accepted what he'd always suspected. She had moved on and was lost to him forever. What did a no-good loser like him have to offer anyone?

He'd tried dating. Tried hooking up with random women. Nothing stirred his blood and made him feel alive, like Elizabeth did. So, when she'd blown back into town in her fancy rental, dressed to kill and looking like some corporate-clad stranger, Peter was shocked by how quickly his mind and body had betrayed him, knocking his heart back a gear and taking off without his permission.

Now he had her back, and by god, it was good! They were older, yes, but the fire between them still burned as hot as ever.

Hasn't the last twelve months proved that?

So what was he waiting for?

Leaping in front of him, Elizabeth startled Peter from his thoughts. "Earth to PJ. You were miles away," she chuckled. "Listen, I'm gonna help Lauren clean up these platters and get them all inside. Then I think we should head off. I think the birthday girl is beat. Maybe give Tommy a hand packing up the chairs and stuff. Your mum and Johnno are heading off too." Elizabeth dropped a chaste kiss on his lips and headed for the mangled platters; bits of food and empty cans littered the table.

Wondering when everyone started leaving, Peter rose to say his farewells. Waving off his mother and brother, he began stacking chairs, tidying as he went.

Lifting the last chair into place, Peter noticed Elizabeth through the kitchen window. Her hands rested on Lauren's stomach. Her eyes lit up excitedly and the two women smiled.

Peter staggered back a step. His heart raced as he steadied himself against the pile of chairs.

"You okay, bud?" Tommy shook Peter by the shoulder.

"Yeah. I think so."

Peter knew he hadn't fooled Tommy. They

knew each other too well. "Do you think you and Lolly will ever get married?"

"Random. Um, probably. I can't imagine my life without her, so why wouldn't I? When we found out she was pregnant though, well... I guess that became our focus. We knew we wanted more space for when the little dude arrives, so it was more important for us to find a house, then spend our money on a wedding, you know?"

"Yeah, yeah. Sure. That makes sense."

"Why?" Tommy looked over to the kitchen window and then back to his friend. He smiled with surprise. "Are you... are you guys pregnant, too?"

"Huh? Oh! God no! No, nothing like that."

"Oh, wow! You're gonna pop the question, aren't you?" Tommy grinned, confident he'd guessed correctly.

"What? No! I... I was just curious about you two. With the baby coming and everything." Peter backtracked.

"Hey, man, whatever. I think it's awesome. You pair were made for each other, seriously."

"You don't think it's too soon?"

"What is too soon? You've been pining after Beth since we were kids. Do it! Then have a baby so we can all be tired old farts together." Tommy laughed.

Peter, however, thought the idea of watching

their kids play together while they all sat drinking coffee under Tommy and Lauren's pergola sounded a little too nice. *Am I really ready for that? Are* we?

In the car, Elizabeth rubbed her shoulder as they made their way back to Peter's apartment. She hadn't officially moved in, but she spent more nights than not at his place these days.

"Sore neck?"

"Yeah. Just a bit tired. Somebody kept me awake last night." She grinned.

"Oh? Oh, I'm sorry. Were they moans of protest I was hearing? Now here I was thinking 'don't stop' meant you wanted me to keep going! Don't worry... I'll be sure to stop next time so you can get plenty of sleep." Peter side-eyed her teasingly.

"You wouldn't dare!"

Peter's eyes left the road to pin her with a look of challenge. *Oh really?*

"No, no! I take that back! Please don't ever stop."

He laughed as he pulled in and killed the engine.

Peter groaned as he laid back on the couch. He should go and shower before he got too comfortable. Before he'd summoned the energy though, Elizabeth moved towards him in nothing but the sexy lace he'd admired that morning. She shifted his leg to straddle his bulk. *Fuck, she is incredible.*

Rubbing herself against the front of his jeans, he could feel her warmth seeping through and hell if it wasn't the sexiest thing he'd ever seen. His cock was so hard it hurt, trapped within the rigid material.

Elizabeth ran one manicured nail down the middle of his shirt. He sucked in a breath as it reached the waist of his pants.

With two calloused hands, he grabbed her peachy round ass cheeks and hoisted her up to taste her sweetness. The lace was wet with her arousal, turning Peter on even more. He had to have her. All of her.

Lowering her back down, Peter made sure to go painfully slow, knowing it drove her wild. He licked a slow wet trail up her skin from her waist to her breasts, where he took his time to indulge each of them. Nipping her budded nipples, she let out a whimper. He kissed the soft underside of her breast, feeling the weight of it against his cheek as he scraped his stubble along each crease. She moaned and gasped as he held her body prisoner and teased her flesh.

"Fuck, PJ. I so badly want to cum. You always tease me until I'm ready to scream. I need you inside me. Please. Now." Elizabeth moaned again with desire.

Peter slid down along the couch, dragging her

with him, but keeping her exactly where he wanted her.

"PJ, please. God. Need you. Need you inside me. Right now." Her words were choppy with hunger.

Peter's cock continued to throb, bound tightly within his jeans, but he refused to free himself until he'd heard her cry out and come undone for him. He slid further down the lounge. An ass cheek in each hand. "Fuck you're sexy, baby. My cock is dripping; I want you so bad. Are you wet for me too?"

"You know I am. Wanna see?" Flopping her head forward to look into his eyes, she pulled the lace aside, giving Peter a clear view of her swollen and glistening sex. He groaned.

"Gonna eat you out until you cum on my face," he grunted before burying himself beneath her.

It wasn't long before Elizabeth's body jolted, and she screamed out her release. Peter smiled against her, giving her apex one last flick with his tongue, and feeling her body shudder in response. Peter knew the moment she had ridden the last of her orgasm. Her attention turned to him. It was his turn. And he had no complaints about that.

Lying naked and spent on the couch together, Peter and Elizabeth's kisses shifted from carnal ones to that of softer, more sensual ones.

She was completely right for him. She matched his energy. His wild and sometimes reckless ways. She pushed back against his stubbornness and challenged him when he needed a jolt.

Peter still couldn't believe she was back for good. To be with him. Having her here, in his arms, Peter knew there would never be another for him. Hadn't his longing for all those years she was gone proven that? No, she was definitely the only woman he had or would ever love. She was *home*.

"Bee?" He whispered the nickname against her temple.

"Yeah?"

"You know how much I love you, right?" He leaned back to look into her eyes. To see that she truly knew. A playful smirk tipped up a corner of her perky lips.

"I certainly hope so. I don't let just anyone hold me hostage while I cum on their face, you know?" Her smile grew. Her eyes reigniting with desire.

God, she is insatiable.

"Be mine. Forever, Bee."

"Always." She shuffled, angling for better access to him.

"I'm serious, Bee. Marry me?"

"What?" Elizabeth paused.

"Marry me? There's not a single person I would

rather travel this wild road with. We're a team. We always have been, and I always want to be. If you want that, too?"

"Are you serious, PJ" Elizabeth climbed to straddle his waist, spearing him with wide eyes of surprise.

"I've never been more serious about anything. Well… Except having you ride my face. That's serious business too." Peter grinned cheekily.

Elizabeth's jaw dropped open as she gave him a half-hearted slap on the shoulder. Mockingly, he flinched away from her sudden attack.

"Don't be vulgar, mister… or you're going to see a whole lot less of it."

"Hah, you're hornier than I am, baby. And you love riding me, so don't pretend you could give it up because we both know you'd never last." He grabbed her wrists and pulled her down on top of him. Their faces only an inch apart. "Marry me, Bee? Make me yours forever."

"I thought you'd never ask." She kissed him passionately until they both needed to regain their breath.

"So… Is that a, yes?"

"Yes! Yes, PJ. Nothing could make me happier than loving you wholly and solely for the rest of forever."

With a heart full of joy and his feisty woman perched on top of him, Peter kissed her with a fierceness like never before. She was everything he'd dared to dream about, and now all those dreams had come true.

Like this story?

You might like J.H. Nelson's latest novel
Upon Butterfly Wings.

Not more.
Not less.
Just different.

"The lights are too bright. I'm surrounded by drunks. Oh, and I'm wearing a dress! Can things really get any worse?"

Danielle has given up on the world. Being autistic makes navigating social events uncomfortable and overwhelming. Why won't her family just leave her alone to read her books in peace, where she is happy and life makes sense?

At his cousin's wedding, it isn't the happy couple that Kevin can't take his eyes off. It's the bride's sister. She isn't like the other girls he's met. Unable to get her out of his mind, Kevin is determined to know her better.

Their differences have drawn them together, but will they also be what tears them apart?